Walls, Brawls, and the Great Rebellion

Walls, Brawls, and the Great Rebellion

Library of Congress Cataloging-in-Publication Data

Lee, Young Shin.

Walls, brawls, and the great rebellion / edited by Brett Burner and J.S. Earls ; original story and art by Young Shin Lee and Jung Sun Hwang.

p. cm. -- (The manga Bible ; bk. 2)

ISBN-13: 978-0-310-71288-6 (softcover)

ISBN-10: 0-310-71288-2 (softcover)

1. Bible stories, English--O.T. I. Burner, Brett A., 1969- II. Earls, J. S. III. Hwang, Jung Sun. IV. Title.

BS551.3.L43 2007

221.9'505--dc22

2007011134

Requests for information should be addressed to: Grand Rapids, Michigan 49530

This book published in conjunction with Lamp Post, Inc.; 8367 Lemon Avenue, La Mesa, CA 91941

Series Editor: Bud Rogers
Managing Editor: Bruce Nuffer
Managing Art Director: Sarah Molegraaf

Printed in United States
08 09 10 11 • 7 6 5 4 3

Walls, Brawls, and the Great Rebellion

Numbers–Joshua–Judges–Ruth

Series Editor: Bud Rogers
Story by Young Shin Lee
Art by Jung Sun Hwang

ZONDERVAN.com/
AUTHORTRACKER
follow your favorite authors

THIS BEAT-UP BOAT WON'T STOP ME. COME ON ALONG AND GRAB AN OAR. OUR BIBLE VOYAGE CONTINUES, WITH MANY MORE TALES IN STORE.
JUDGES
RUTH
JOSHUA
NUMBERS

NUMBERS

HEY AARON, HOW CAN MOSES HAVE A CUSHITE WIFE? IS HE CRAZY?!
WHY IS MY EAR ITCHING?
HE MUST BE CRAZY. GOD SHOULD USE US MORE INSTEAD. WE'RE SPECIAL TOO.

AARON, MIRIAM, AND MOSES, COME TO THE MEETING TENT.

I LOVE MOSES BECAUSE HE IS THE MOST FAITHFUL. YOU SHOULD BE AFRAID TO SPEAK AGAINST MOSES.

!

AARON, WHAT'S GOING ON??!!

EEK! I HAVE LEPROUS SORES ALL OVER!!
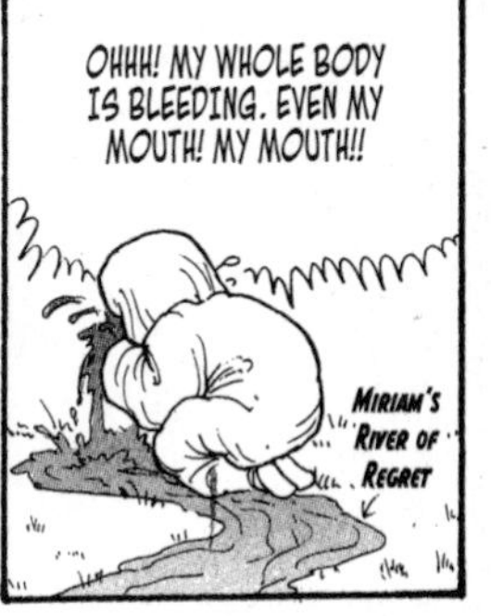
OHHH! MY WHOLE BODY IS BLEEDING. EVEN MY MOUTH! MY MOUTH!!
MIRIAM'S RIVER OF REGRET

GOD, PLEASE FORGIVE MY SISTER, MIRIAM, AND HEAL HER SICKNESS!
OHHH! GOD, I WILL NEVER SPEAK AGAINST YOUR SERVANT AGAIN! PLEASE FORGIVE ME. PLEASE ...!

PITCH A TENT IN THE DESERT AND LOCK HER IN. IF SHE REPENTS AFTER SEVEN DAYS, LET HER OUT.

GOD, PLEASE FORGIVE ME! OHHHHH ...!
MIRIAM'S SEA OF SORROW

GOD HAS MADE ME CLEAN AFTER SEVEN DAYS OF PRAYER! I WILL NEVER SPEAK AGAINST MY BROTHER MOSES AGAIN!!

AFTER LEAVING EGYPT MANY MONTHS AGO, WE HAVE FINALLY REACHED THE LAND OF CANAAN!

IS EVERYONE HERE?

YES, SIR! WE'RE ALL HERE, SIR!!

OKAY! YOU TWELVE LEADERS OF THE TRIBES, GO AND INSPECT THE LAND OF CANAAN. GIVE A THOROUGH REPORT, AND BRING BACK SOME FRUIT FROM THE LAND.

AND YOU IN THE FRONT!
ME?

ARE YOU FILMING A MOVIE?! TAKE OFF YOUR SUNGLASSES AND THAT FAKE MUSTACHE!!

AFTER FORTY DAYS ...
LOOK! THE SPIES WE SENT ARE COMING BACK!!

CANAAN MISSION REPORT
HURRY, TELL US! IS IT A GOOD LAND TO LIVE IN?
WHAT SORT OF PEOPLE LIVE IN THE LAND?

INDEED, THE LAND IS GOOD, BUT BIG, SCARY PEOPLE LIVE THERE.
WE'RE LIKE ITTY-BITTY GRASSHOPPERS NEXT TO THOSE GIANTS ...!

OHHH! WE'VE COME SO FAR, ONLY TO BE SQUISHED BY GIANTS!
I DON'T WANT TO BE SQUISHED ...

HEY! LET'S GO BACK TO EGYPT!
LET'S FIRE MOSES AND AARON AND GET NEW LEADERS!!
MO MUST GO!

HOW CAN YOU SAY THAT?!? IT'S A LAND FLOWING WITH MILK AND HONEY!!

PEOPLE, LOOK AT THESE GRAPES I BROUGHT BACK! THEY'RE SO BIG, GROWN MEN HAVE TO CARRY THEM! GOD HAS PROMISED TO GIVE THIS LAND TO US!!

WE WILL WIN BECAUSE GOD IS WITH US! HOW STRONG CAN THESE PEOPLE BE? LET'S ATTACK!!

I WILL GIVE THE LAND I PROMISED TO THE PEOPLE OF ISRAEL, BUT YOU WILL WANDER THE DESERT FOR FORTY YEARS. ALL THE PEOPLE WHO CAME OUT OF EGYPT WILL DIE, BUT THEIR CHILDREN SHALL GROW UP AND ENTER CANAAN.

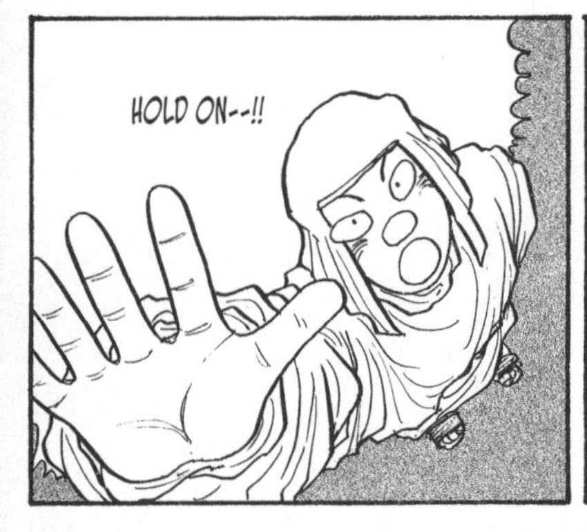
HOLD ON--!!

FORGET WHAT WE SAID. WE'LL ATTACK CANAAN!!

LET'S GO!!
MOSES, PLEASE PRAY FOR US!
C'MON!

HEY! GOD HAS ALREADY DECIDED! IT'S TOO LATE!
RUMBLE!
ATTACK!

OY VEY! KIDS ...
RETREAT!
RETREAT!

TOTAL DEFEAT! I EVEN BROKE MY ARM ...!!
THAT'S IT! WE'RE FINISHED! KA-PUT! DONE FOR ...!

MR. DATHAN! MOSES IS A TOTAL DICTATOR! WITH ONE WORD HE KILLS OR SAVES US.
YOU'RE RIGHT, KORAH! IS MOSES A KING? WE'RE ALSO HOLY, AND GOD IS WITH US TOO!

TRIBAL LEADERS! IF WE BECOME RULERS WE SHALL UNITE AND CREATE A DEMOCRACY. VOTE FOR KORAH AND DATHAN!
VOTE! VOTE!
"NO MORE MO!"

GO!
NO MORE MO!
NO!
No Mo!
Mo Must Go!

GOD SHALL DECIDE THIS MATTER. TOMORROW WE'LL BRING HIM INCENSE. GOD WILL CHOOSE WHO STAYS AND WHO GOES.
YEA! THE TIME HAS COME!

GOD, I'VE BROUGHT THE LIGHTED INCENSE ...
STEP ASIDE, MOSES! I SHALL DESTROY THEM!

ISRAELITES! MOVE AWAY FROM THE TENTS OF KORAH AND DATHAN!!
?
? ?

EARTHQUAKE!
SAVE US!
AHH!
C-C-RACK!
쩌억

쿠르릉
KA-BOOM!
SAVE ME!

KORAH, DATHAN, AND TWO HUNDRED FIFTY LEADERS WERE KILLED!

COME OUT HERE LEADER-KILLER!
KILL MOSES!

MOSES AND AARON, LEAVE THESE PEOPLE SO I MAY DESTROY THEM.
!
!

GASP!
SO DIZZY!

PLAGUE ...
I ... I CAN'T BREATHE!

GOD, PLEASE FORGIVE THESE PEOPLE'S SIN OF DISOBEDIENCE ...!

THE PLAGUE IS GONE.
BUT OVER FOURTEEN THOUSAND PEOPLE HAVE DIED ...!

NOW, GATHER THE STAFFS OF THE TWELVE TRIBES AND PLACE THEM BESIDE THE ARK IN THE TENT OF MEETING. I WILL SHOW THE PEOPLE WHO I CHOOSE BY MAKING A STAFF GROW LEAVES.

AARON'S STAFF HAS SPROUTED. IT HAS EVEN PRODUCED ALMONDS ...!

I WILL PUT IT WITH THE ARK!

WE'VE BEEN WALKING IN THE DESERT FOR A LONG TIME WITHOUT WATER.
OOOH ... I'M TIRED!

C'MON! TAKE US BACK TO EGYPT!
MOSES' MAGIC TRICKED US!
YEAH! WHERE WE CAN EAT AND DRINK!!

SQUISH!
SLITHER!

AAAAAAAAH! SNAKES!!

HEY! THE SNAKE WHO BITES THE MOST PEOPLE WINS!

I GOT 19!
22!
12!
WOW!

MY TEETH ARE WORN OUT BECAUSE I BIT SO MANY.
I KNOW A GOOD DENTIST!

MOSES! WE MADE A MISTAKE COMPLAINING ABOUT YOU. THE SNAKES HAVE KILLED SO MANY! PLEASE SAVE US ...

GET ALL OUR BRONZE, MAKE A SNAKE, AND PUT IT ON A POLE. IF A VICTIM LOOKS AT IT, GOD WILL HEAL HIM OR HER.

I WAS HEALED WHEN I LOOKED AT THE BRONZE SNAKE.
IT'S A MIRACLE!
YEA!
EXCUSE ME ... I'M A POLE-VAULTER. HAVE YOU SEEN MY POLE?
UH, SORRY ...
THIS ONE'S DIFFERENT. IT'S PRETTY ... AND IT HEALS PEOPLE!
THE LAST TIME I LOOKED AT A SNAKE IT BIT ME!

HE COULD HAVE BEEN CURED!
IF GOD SAID IT, IT'S GOOD ENOUGH FOR ME!
WHAT HAVE WE GOT TO LOSE? WE'RE DYING ANYWAY!

IT'S BEEN FORTY YEARS SINCE WE LEFT EGYPT. I'M ONE HUNDRED TWENTY YEARS OLD NOW. MY SISTER, MIRIAM, AND BROTHER, AARON, HAVE DIED. THE CHILDREN WERE TAUGHT THE WORD OF GOD AND ARE STRONG!!

WHAT BRINGS YOU HERE?
OUR KING HAS SENT THESE GIFTS FOR YOU, BALAAM.

TOUGH TIMES IN THE BIG CITY, EH? WAIT THE NIGHT AND I SHALL PRAY ...

GOD, GIVE ME A WORD AGAINST THE ISRAELITES.
I HAVE BLESSED THE ISRAELITES. DO NOT CURSE THEM! AND DO NOT GO WITH THESE STRANGERS.
I THOUGHT YOU'D SAY THAT ...

GOD TOLD ME NOT TO JOIN YOU.
UM, BALAAM SAYS HE WON'T COME.
HMMM ... DID WE NOT GIVE HIM ENOUGH? TAKE MORE GIFTS AND OFFER HIM A GOOD JOB WITH GREAT BENEFITS.

WOW!

MORE GIFTS?
GREAT JOB?!
HERE YA GO!

HI-YO DONKEY!
WEALTH AND
POWER AWAITS!

STOP!
AN ANGEL!

ARE YOU DEAF? STAY
ON THE ROAD!
IS HE
BLIND?

YOU BETTER SHAPE
UP!!
WHAP!

LET'S GO, DONKEY!

NO WAY!

URK!

YOU BANGED ME INTO A WALL AND HURT ME!!
... I DIDN'T MEAN TO ...!

THIS'LL KNOCK SOME SENSE INTO YOU!!

NOW KNOCK IT OFF!

IT'S NO USE. MEN NEVER LISTEN ...
DO YOU HAVE RABIES OR SOMETHING ...?

OH NO! NOT AGAIN!

?
WE'RE DOOMED! DOOMED!

THAT'S IT! YOU'RE GOING TO THE VET!
AND YOU'RE GOING TO THE BARBER!

OKAY, DONKEY-BOY! LET'S GET IT ON!

COME HERE!!

SLAM!
FLY THE FRIENDLY SKIES!!

OOOOH ...
THAT'S IT! I CAN'T TAKE IT ANYMORE!

OKAY, OKAY! PUNCHING I CAN UNDERSTAND, BUT THE SIDE ROUNDHOUSE KICK AND REVERSE THROW?! HOW CAN YOU DO THAT TO ME? I'M DEPENDABLE AND GREAT ON GAS! THINK OF ALL OUR GOOD TIMES ...!
LISTEN, YOU'RE A DONKEY. YOU CAN'T TALK.

LOOK AT ME, I DON'T EVEN KNOW WHY I'M TALKING TO YOU ...!
PLEASE! HAVE I EVER DISOBEYED YOU BEFORE?

LET ME THINK ...

HEY!
AN ANGEL!

WHY DID YOU HIT THE DONKEY? YOU WERE GOING THE WRONG WAY! IF THE DONKEY DIDN'T STOP ... YOU'D BE DEAD!
I'LL GO BACK HOME.

NO, KEEP GOING NOW, BUT DON'T EVEN THINK ABOUT CURSING THE ISRAELITES!
OKAY! OKAY!

WELCOME, GREAT PROPHET!
I'M GOING TO DO WHATEVER GOD SAYS.

I PREPARED SEVEN ALTARS WITH SEVEN CALVES. NOW, CURSE THE ISRAELITES.

GOD, I CAN'T CURSE YOUR PEOPLE. PLEASE BLESS THEM!!

NO, NO, NO. YOU'RE SUPPOSED TO CURSE THEM, NOT BLESS THEM!
LET'S TRY A DIFFERENT MOUNTAIN.

GOD, DO NOT TAKE BACK YOUR BLESSINGS!

HEY, HOW CAN YOU DO THIS?!?
I CAN'T DO ANYTHING ABOUT IT.
THIS IS GOD'S WILL!!
END OF NUMBERS

JOSHUA

MOSES! YOUR DEATH IS NEAR! CHOOSE JOSHUA TO REPLACE YOU ...
YES, GOD!

MEETING
ANNOUNCER:
MOSES
AGENDA:
IMPORTANT STUFF
LOCATION:
TO BE ANNOUNCED
?
?

BY GOD'S COMMAND ... JOSHUA IS MY SUCCESSOR!!
HE WILL LEAD YOU INTO CANAAN!

I WILL DIE HERE AND WILL NOT ENTER CANAAN, AS GOD COMMANDED.

I AM FINALLY GOING TO THE KINGDOM OF GOD ...

OHHH ...!
MOSES!
WE'LL MISS HIM SO MUCH!!

MOSES HAS PASSED AWAY, AND I HAVE NO STRENGTH. HOW CAN I TAKE CANAAN?

GOD, GIVE ME STRENGTH.
JOSHUA! DO NOT BE AFRAID! I WILL BE WITH YOU AS I WAS WITH MOSES. OBEY ALL MY LAWS AND YOU WILL BE SUCCESSFUL IN WHATEVER YOU DO.

THREE DAYS FROM NOW WE WILL CROSS THE RIVER OF JORDAN AND TAKE OUR LAND!!

THERE ARE MANY SOLDIERS IN JERICHO AND ITS WALLS ARE HIGH, BUT GOD WILL GIVE IT TO US.
YAY!
YEAH!
WE BELIEVE!

JOSHUA, I HAVE BROUGHT TWO PEOPLE WHO WILL BE SPIES.
LET THEM IN!

WE'RE READY FOR OUR SECRET MISSION!!
QUIET DOWN. JERICHO MIGHT HEAR!

WE FINISHED SPYING. NOW, WHERE ARE WE SLEEPING?
THERE'S AN AD HERE FOR ...

RAHAB'S PLACE
VACANCY - FREE CABLE
HELLO?!

WHAT CAN I GET YOU?
WE'RE NOT HERE FOR DRINK. HERE'S SOME GOLD FOR FOOD AND A PLACE TO SLEEP.

OH MY! GO UPSTAIRS TO ROOM 77.

HEY, THOSE DUDES LOOKED LIKE SPIES.
LET'S TELL THE KING ...

SPIES FROM ISRAEL? MOBILIZE SWAT AND SURROUND RAHAB'S PLACE.

YOU'RE SURROUNDED! COME OUT WITH YOUR HANDS UP!!!

UH-OH ... WE ARE SOOO BUSTED!
GOD, HELP US!

WHAM!
HEY SPY GUYS, YOU CAN HIDE UPSTAIRS!

WHY ARE YOU HELPING US? YOU'RE FROM JERICHO.
!

I'LL TELL YOU LATER! HURRY!

I'M AFRAID OF THE DARK.
I'M MORE AFRAID OF DEATH.

WHAT'S GOING ON, OFFICER?
YOU DON'T KNOW?! WE'RE HERE TO ARREST THE SPIES WHO CAME HERE!

WHAT?! THEY JUST LEFT! I THINK THEY WERE HEADED FOR THE CITY GATE BEFORE IT CLOSED!

ALL OF YOU, TO THE GATE! SHOOT FIRST, ASK QUESTIONS LATER!

THEY'RE GONE. YOU CAN COME OUT NOW.

WHY DID YOU RISK YOUR LIFE TO SAVE US?
I KNOW HOW GOD BROUGHT YOU OUT OF EGYPT AND PARTED THE RED SEA. AND I KNOW GOD WILL GIVE YOU THIS CITY.

GREAT! SO WHAT CAN WE DO FOR YOU?
PLEASE SPARE MY FAMILY WHEN YOU DEFEAT THIS CITY.

WE WILL. GATHER YOUR FAMILY AND HANG A RED ROPE OUTSIDE YOUR WINDOW.

BE CAREFUL, THE COPS ARE STILL AFTER YOU. HIDE IN THE MOUNTAINS FOR THREE DAYS, THEN RUN AWAY.

WHEW! WE BARELY MADE IT!
FINALLY, THEY'RE GIVING UP. LET'S LEAVE.

WHAT TOOK YOU SO LONG? WE THOUGHT YOU WERE CAPTURED.
THIS NICE GIRL NAMED RAHAB HELPED US!

MAKE SURE YOU TELL OUR PEOPLE NOT TO ATTACK HER HOUSE!

MARCH TOWARD THE CITY OF JERICHO!!

THE WATER IS PARTING!
THE SAME THING HAPPENED WITH THE RED SEA FORTY YEARS AGO!
NEED WATER!
CAN'T BREATHE...!

THANK YOU, GOD, FOR HELPING US CROSS ...

ARE YOU OUR FRIEND OR OUR FOE?

NEITHER. I AM THE COMMANDER OF GOD'S ARMY.

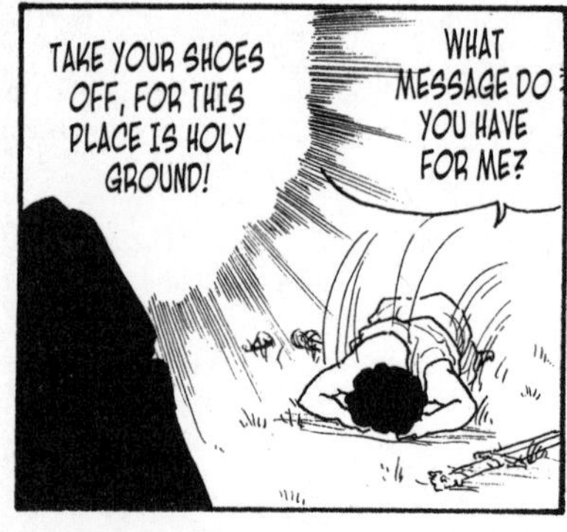
TAKE YOUR SHOES OFF, FOR THIS PLACE IS HOLY GROUND!
WHAT MESSAGE DO YOU HAVE FOR ME?

PLACE THE ARK BEFORE YOU, AND WITH TRUMPETS BLOWING, HAVE THE PEOPLE MARCH AROUND THE CITY ONCE A DAY FOR SIX DAYS. ON THE SEVENTH DAY, MARCH AROUND THE CITY SEVEN TIMES, AND THEN YOU SHALL ALL SHOUT.

DO THIS AND THE CITY OF JERICHO WILL FALL.

?

JOSHUA, IS EVERYTHING OKAY?
SORRY! LITTLE SLEEPY!

GOD WANTS US TO CIRCLE THE CITY ONCE A DAY WITH THE ARK BEFORE US.
YES, SIR! IF IT'S GOD'S COMMAND, WE'LL DO IT!

TOOT! TOOT! TA-TA TOOT!

HEY, LOOK AT THE SIXTH TRUMPET GUY. ISN'T HE HANDSOME?!
THE SEVENTH GUY'S DREAMY!!
THEY'RE SO COOL!!!
TOOT! TOOT! TA-TA TOOT!

WE LOVE YOU JOSH!
WE LOVE ♥ JOSH!! XXOXXOO
TOOT! TOOT! TA-TA TOOT!

I'M GOING TO CRY!
PLAY THAT HORN!!
I LOVE HIM!!
WE LOVE ♥ JOSH!! XXOXXOO
BA-TA TOOT! TA-TA TOOT!

HEY! WHAT ARE YOU DOING?! YOU'RE NOT SUPPOSED TO CHEER FOR THE ENEMY!!!
TOOT! TOOT! TA-TA TOOT!

HOW LONG ARE THEY GONNA DO THIS?
CRAZY BAND GEEKS!
SO SLEEPY ...
TOOT! TA-TA TOOT! RA-TA BA-TA TOOT! TOOT!

THIS IS IT. THE SEVENTH DAY!

ATTACK!!!

YAAAAAAAAAY! YAAAAAAAAY! YAAAAAAAAAY!

THE WALL'S FALLING!
C-R-EEEEAK!

BOOM!

THESE PEOPLE WORSHIP FALSE GODS. WE MUST DESTROY THEM OR WE SHALL FALL AWAY FROM GOD AS WELL!

AT THAT TIME, ALL THE PEOPLE IN THE CITY OF JERICHO WERE KILLED--EVEN THE LIVESTOCK. ONLY RAHAB'S FAMILY WAS SPARED.

BUT WHY? WHY DID GOD COMMAND SUCH DESTRUCTION OF LIFE??

SOME TRIBES IN CANAAN BURNED THEIR OWN CHILDREN AS A SACRIFICE TO THEIR FALSE GODS. GOD USED THE ISRAELITES TO PUNISH THOSE TRIBES.
WHAM!

GOD ALSO DID THIS TO PROTECT ISRAEL FROM WICKED RELIGION AND SIN.
BROTHER!

THE DRY CLEANER WANTS YOU TO RETURN THE SUIT YOU BORROWED! HURRY UP!
OKAY, OKAY!

OHHH! WHEN AM I GONNA HAVE A NICE SUIT?!?
RIVER OF POVERTY
THERE'S A STAIN ON IT!

BRING ALL THE GOLD AND TREASURES YOU FIND IN THE CITY TO ME! THEY BELONG TO GOD!

NO ONE'S WATCHING? I, ACHAN, SHALL HIDE THESE TREASURES FOR MYSELF ...!

NOW WE WILL ATTACK THE CITY OF AI. IT IS A SMALL CITY. THREE THOUSAND SOLDIERS SHOULD BE ENOUGH TO WIN.

BUT THAT WAS NOT THE CASE ...
OOOOH! WE ARE DEFEATED!
ARGH! I BROKE MY LEG!

GOD, WHY DID YOU LET US LOSE??
HOW CAN I HELP WHEN ONE OF YOUR PEOPLE HAS STOLEN FROM ME?

LORD, SHOW ME WHO DID THIS!!

I HAVE COMMITTED A TERRIBLE SIN.
I HID SOME OF THE TREASURE.

FOR THAT, TROUBLE WILL COME ON YOU TODAY. STONE ACHAN AND BURN THE TREASURE!!

NOW GOD WILL BE WITH US. FOLLOW ME TO AI!

THEY'RE COMING BACK? EVEN THOUGH WE WON LAST TIME? I DON'T THINK THEY LEARNED THEIR LESSON!

THEY'RE COMING AFTER US!
GO! GET 'EM!
YAAY!
LET'S RUN!
ATTACK THE ISRAELITES!

WE'LL DEFEAT YOU A SECOND TIME!!

THE PLAN WORKED. THEY DIDN'T SEE US HIDING HERE!
THE CITY'S EMPTY. LET'S BURN IT DOWN!!

OH NO! THEY TRICKED US! OUR CITY'S ON FIRE!

THIS IS THE ISRAELITE ARMY THAT RAN AWAY ...
TODAY'S MENU
AI SANDWICH

THIS IS THE ISRAELITE ARMY THAT WAS BURNING THE CITY ...

THIS IS THE ARMY OF AI WHO WERE CHASING THE FIRST ISRAELITE ARMY ...
FRIED EGG

AND THAT'S HOW YOU MAKE AN AI SANDWICH!
TIPS WELCOME

WE HAVE CONQUERED AI AND JERICHO!!

THE ARMY OF ISRAEL BEAT THE ARMIES OF JERICHO AND AI!
THE CITY OF GIBEON IS MIGHTY, BUT THEY WILL DESTROY US IN NO TIME!

CAN WE SAVE OURSELVES?
I DON'T WANT TO DIE!
I DON'T EVEN WANNA FIGHT ...
CONFERENCE ROOM

GENTLEMEN, WE HAVE TO TRICK THE PEOPLE OF ISRAEL.
SOUNDS GOOD TO ME!

WE NEED WORN SHOES, OLD CLOTHES, STALE PIZZA, AND FLAT SODA ...!

WHEN ISRAEL SEES US WITH THESE THINGS, THEY'LL THINK OUR CITY IS TOO FAR AWAY TO ATTACK. THEN, THEY'LL SIGN A PEACE TREATY WITH US.

WOW! YOU'RE A GENIUS!
YOU'RE A BORN LIAR ... ER ... LAWYER ... I MEAN ... LEADER!

IS THIS WHERE THE FAMOUS COMMANDER JOSHUA IS STAYING?
YES. FOLLOW ME, WEARY, WORN-OUT, WANDERING ONE.
OH! I'M SO TIRED! THAT WAS A LONG JOURNEY ...!
YOUR ACCENT IS LOCAL. WHY ARE YOU SAYING YOU CAME FROM FAR AWAY?

WE HAVE COME FROM A LAND FAR, FAR AWAY TO MAKE A TREATY WITH YOU. YOU PROBABLY HAVEN'T EVEN HEARD OF OUR LAND. IT'S CALLED GIBEON. RING A BELL? DIDN'T THINK SO ...

GIBEON?

WE CAME SO FAR OUR PIZZA GOT ALL STALE AND SQUISHY. SEE? AND JUST LOOK AT OUR CLOTHES!

ALL RIGHT, YOU CAN STAY AND SERVE US IF YOU WANT. WE WON'T KILL YOU.
YES!

OUR LIVES ARE SAVED!
GOOD JOB! YOU'RE THE MAN!

WHAT! YOU SAY GIBEON'S RIGHT NEXT DOOR? ERRRRR ...!

BUT, I PROMISED THEM THEY COULD BE OUR SERVANTS AND WE'D LET THEM LIVE ...!

WHAT? GIBEON BETRAYED US AMORITES AND SIDED WITH ISRAEL?
WE MUST UNITE TO SURVIVE. LET'S JOIN UP!
LET'S ATTACK GIBEON FIRST!!

IT'S THE AMORITE COALITION!
ATTACK!
ATTACK!

WHAT ARE WE GOING TO DO?!
CHILL! THIS IS WHY WE MADE THE PEACE TREATY WITH ISRAEL!

FINE! YOU'RE JUST LUCKY I SPEAK THE TRUTH! UNLIKE YOU!
PLEASE HELP US POOR GIBEONITES ...

THE ARMY OF ISRAEL HAS COME TO HELP US!!
THE ARMY OF ISRAEL HAS ARRIVED!!
IT'S THE ARMY OF ISRAEL!! LET'S SPLIT!
MOMMY!

GO! DESTROY THE AMORITES!
LEGS DON'T FAIL ME!
MOVE IT!

OWWW! THE SKY IS FALLING!
IT'S HAILING!

GOD IS HELPING ISRAEL ...!

WE'RE NOT FINISHED FIGHTING, BUT THE SUN IS SETTING!
WHEN IT GETS DARK, THE AMORITE ARMY WILL HIDE! WHAT SHOULD WE DO?
OH, THE AGONY!

HMMM ... THEN I WILL ASK GOD TO KEEP THE SUN AND THE MOON IN THEIR PLACE.

SUN, STOP MOVING!!

OY VEY! I HAVE TO OBEY THAT PUNY LITTLE HUMAN DOWN THERE?!?
OKAY GOD. WHATEVER YOU SAY. YOU'RE THE BOSS!

SO JOSHUA CONTINUED TO CONQUER THE CITIES IN THE LAND FOR ISRAEL.

YOUR MISSION, SHOULD YOU ACCEPT IT, IS TO SNEAK INTO THE OTHER LANDS AND MAKE MAPS ...
YES, SIR!

WE'RE BACK SAFELY WITH THE MAPS!
THEN I WILL DIVIDE THE LAND BY ROLLING DICE.

FINALLY, EVERYTHING IS DIVIDED!

JOSHUA, I WILL GIVE YOU THE LAND OF TIMNATH SERAH. YOU WILL LIVE THERE.
OH GOD, THANK YOU!

TIME OUT! GOD ALSO HAD JOSHUA BUILD CITIES OF REFUGE FOR PEOPLE WHO ACCIDENTALLY KILLED SOMEONE TO HIDE IN, BECAUSE RELATIVES WERE SUPPOSED TO KILL MURDERERS.

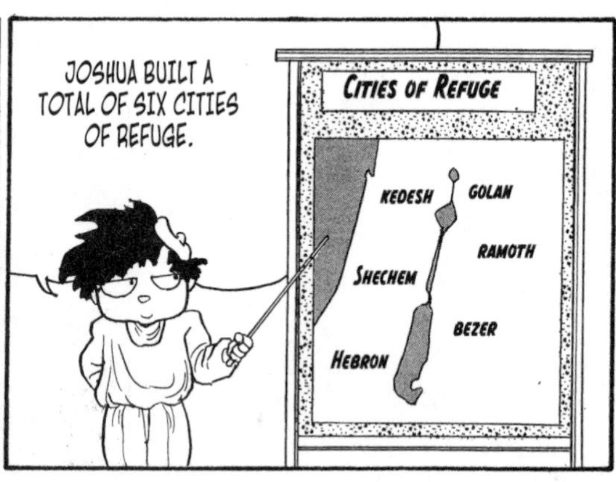
JOSHUA BUILT A TOTAL OF SIX CITIES OF REFUGE.
CITIES OF REFUGE
KEDESH
GOLAN
RAMOTH
SHECHEM
BEZER
HEBRON

THIRTY YEARS LATER ...
GATHER THE LEADERS OF THE TWELVE TRIBES TO THE LAND OF SHECHEM!

I'M ALREADY ONE HUNDRED TEN YEARS OLD, SO I WANT TO MAKE MY WILL!
WILL YOU CONTINUE TO FOLLOW GOD EVEN AFTER I AM GONE?

WE WILL ONLY SERVE GOD! WE PROMISE!!

I HAVE WRITTEN THIS PROMISE ON THE STONE BENEATH THAT TREE.

OBEY AND KEEP THE LAWS GOD GAVE TO MOSES! DO NOT TURN AWAY FROM THEM!

JOSHUA DIED AT ONE HUNDRED TEN YEARS OLD AND WAS BURIED IN TIMNATH SERAH.
END OF JOSHUA

JUDGES

ISRAEL LOST ITS HEAD HONCHO WHEN JOSHUA DIED.

THEY DID WHAT GOD COMMANDED. STARTING WITH THE TRIBE OF JUDAH ...

... THEY INVADED THE LAND OF CANAAN. BUT IT WAS A STRUGGLE ...

THE JUDGES WERE RAISED UP BY THE LORD TO SAVE ISRAEL FROM ITS ENEMIES. GOD WOULD LEAD THEM TO VICTORY.

AS GOD COMMANDED, DO NOT LEAVE ANY SURVIVORS!!

LET'S RUMBLE!

WAIT, WAIT A MINUTE ...!

PLEASE! SAVE ME THIS ONCE! IF I WERE ALONE, WOULD I BEG LIKE THIS? I DON'T THINK SO! I'VE GOT AN EIGHTY-YEAR-OLD MOTHER AND THREE LITTLE KIDS. IF I DIE, THEY'LL ALL DIE OF HUNGER!!!

ARE ... ARE YOU TELLING THE TRUTH ...?

UH-HUH

WHAT'S WRONG?
I WAS GOING TO KILL HIM, BUT LISTEN TO THIS ...

OOOH! THAT IS SO SAD. VERY, VERY SAD!!

IT'S NOT MUCH, BUT I HOPE IT HELPS YOUR FAMILY!
GOOD LUCK, BRO!

LET'S NOT KILL THEM ANYMORE!
YEAH MAN, LET'S HAVE PEACE!
THANK YOU, FRIENDS, THANK YOU!

RING!

RING!
RING!

HI HONEY, IT'S ME. EVERYTHING WORKED ACCORDING TO PLAN. THESE ISRAELITES ARE SUCKERS! YOU SHOULD HAVE AN EASY TIME WITH THEM.

I CERTAINLY SHOULD!

WOW! A CANAANITE WOMAN!!
SHE'S SO PRETTY! I COULD MARRY HER!
IS IT JUST ME, OR IS IT HOT OUT HERE?

I CAN'T TAKE IT ANYMORE!

HEY, BABY!
OH MY!

WANNA GET MARRIED?!
OOH ...!

I'LL GIVE YOU WHATEVER YOU WANT! ICE CREAM! AIR CONDITIONING! ALASKA!!

ALL RIGHT! AND I'LL TEACH YOU HOW WE CANAANITES WORSHIP OUR GOD, BAAL!

YOU DON'T WORSHIP GOD?!

GOD WON'T LIKE THAT ...
NO, BAAL! HE DOESN'T EVEN PUNISH US WHEN WE SIN!

DON'T WORRY, BAAL IS JUST AS POWERFUL.

A BRAVE MAN GETS A PRETTY GIRL! I'VE GOTTA GET ME ONE OF THOSE!

THIS IS BAAL, THE ONE WHO BLESSES US!
HMM, AND HE WON'T PUNISH US WHEN WE SIN?

I LIKE THIS GOD!
HIC-CUP!
THIS IS THE LIFE! WORSHIPING BAAL ROCKS!

WHAT DID YOU SAY? THOSE ISRAELITE FOOLS ARE WORSHIPING BAAL? HA HA!!

MESOPOTAMIAN WARRIORS! LISTEN TO ME, CUSHAN-RISHATHAIM, THE KING OF ARAM NAHARAIM! ISRAEL IS WEAKENED! LET'S DESTROY THEM!!!
YAAAAY! YIPEEE!

WE'RE NOT AFRAID OF ANYONE WHO DOESN'T SERVE BAAL!
ACK! THIS IS THE PRICE WE PAY FOR BETRAYING GOD ...!!

NOW, WE HAVE BEEN RULED BY CUSHAN-RISHATHAIM FOR EIGHT YEARS! GOD, PLEASE FORGIVE US!

OTHNIEL, NEPHEW OF CALEB! I HAVE HEARD THE PRAYERS OF ISRAEL. GO AND SAVE YOUR PEOPLE BY DRIVING OUT THE KING OF ARAM NAHARAIM.

MEN, FOLLOW ME!!

OWEEEE!

WE WON!
PRAISE GOD!
YEA, OTHNIEL!

DURING THE FORTY-YEAR REIGN OF JUDGE OTHNIEL, ISRAEL LIVED IN PEACE.
GOD, YOU ARE ALWAYS WITH US!

BUT WHEN OTHNIEL DIED, PEOPLE SINNED AGAIN ...
LET'S WORSHIP BAAL!
YEAH, WHATEVER!
THAT'S ASHERAH, THE FEMALE GOD!!
SHE'S DEFINITELY BAAL'S "BETTER HALF"!

OH, BAAL AND ASHERAH! PLEASE GRANT US JOY!!

IT'S BEEN SO LONG SINCE I PARTIED!

LISTEN, FELLOW MOABITES! ISRAEL IS WEAKENED! WE HAVE NOTHING TO FEAR!
I, KING EGLON, WILL UNITE THE MOABITES, AMMONITES, AND AMALEKITES AND CONQUER ISRAEL!!

UH-OH ...

WAITER ... SOME MORE WINE, PLEASE?
HA!

MOMMY!
IT'S SO EASY. THEY'RE ALL DRUNK!
ACK!
URK!

HA! NOW, THIS LAND IS MINE! GO SEARCH THE HOUSES AND COLLECT TAXES!!!

IRS! OPEN UP!
BOOM!

GIVE US EVERYTHING! YOU KNOW WHAT'LL HAPPEN IF YOU DON'T!

WE HAVE NOTHING. YOU TOOK EVERYTHING LAST TIME.
WE HAVEN'T EATEN ANYTHING IN A WEEK!

SEARCH THE PLACE!

GOT SOMETHING!
BEEP! BEEP! BEEP!

THERE ARE THREE PIECES OF RICE!

RICE-HOARDER!
POW!

FINE! TAKE THE RICE! THERE'S NOTHING ELSE YOU CAN TAKE!

NOO! NOOOOO!

MY HAIR ...
DEAR, YOU SHOULDN'T HAVE SAID ANYTHING ...

GOD, PLEASE FORGIVE US. WE HAVE BEEN TREATED THIS WAY FOR EIGHTEEN YEARS! GOD, PLEASE?!

EHUD! YOU WILL SAVE THE PEOPLE OF ISRAEL FROM KING EGLON.

I UNDERSTAND GOD, BUT I AM WEAK, AND EGLON HAS A HUGE ARMY.
YOU CAN WIN. BE BRAVE.

I'LL OBEY. I'LL EVEN HIDE THIS KNIFE ON MY LEG ...!

WE ARE HERE TO PAY TRIBUTE TO KING EGLON WITH WINE AND TREASURES!

HA! VERY GOOD! VERY GOOD! I LIKE THE SPARKLY ONES!

THIS IS NOTHING COMPARED TO WHAT I'D REALLY LIKE TO GIVE YOU, MY KING!

I'LL SHOW YOU. BUT THIS IS TOTALLY TOP SECRET ...!

COOL, I LIKE SPY STUFF. LET'S SEE ... WHERE TO TALK? HEY, LET'S GO TO MY ROOM!

OKAY, WHAT'S THE BIG SECRET? WHAT DO YOU HAVE FOR ME?
WHAT I REALLY WANT TO GIVE YOU IS ... MY KNIFE!

GOD TOLD ME TO SLAY YOU.
HA HA! YOU'RE KILLING ME!

HERE'S MY KNIFE ... JUST FOR YOU!
IT REALLY IS A NICE KNIFE, BUT ...

ACK! YOU REALLY ARE KILLING ME ...!
CHUNK!

THE KNIFE'S NOT COMING OUT! HE'S TOO FAT!

I'LL LOCK THE DOOR AND GO OUT THE WINDOW.

PEOPLE OF ISRAEL, I HAVE KILLED KING EGLON!!
LET'S DRIVE OUT THE MOABITES TOGETHER!!
YEAH!
YEAH!
YAY!

ONE GROUP GOES WITH ME. THE OTHER GOES TO JORDAN!!

HEY, WHERE'S THE KING? I HAVE MANY THINGS HE NEEDS TO SIGN!

HE'S STILL NOT OUT?

NOT YET?!

IS HE GOING TO RUN THIS COUNTRY OR WHAT? KNOCK ON THE DOOR!!

KING!! KING!!
BANG! BANG!
TAP TAP TAP

GO GET THE SPARE KEY! I CAN'T WAIT!

GASP! OUR KING IS DEAD ...!

CHARRRGE!
WHAT'S THAT SOUND?
BEATS ME ...

IT'S THE ISRAELITE ARMY!!
AAAAH!

ISRAELITES IN FRONT AND A DEAD KING BEHIND ...
ATTACK! ATTACK!

AND WE'RE STUCK IN THE MIDDLE ...?
KILL! MAIM!

I DON'T THINK SO! RUN FOR MOAB!!
ZOOM!

THE ROAD TO MOAB IS JUST ACROSS THE RIVER JORDAN ...
WE'RE LUCKY TO BE ALIVE. MOST OF THE OTHERS WERE KILLED BY THE ISRAELITES ...!

HEY, YOU'RE LATE FOR YOUR WHUPPIN'!
WHO'S THIS DUDE?

WE'RE ESCAPING, BUT WHAT CAN YOU DO AGAINST SO MANY ...?

WELL, LET'S FIND OUT ...
OH, SUPER SOLDIERS!!

THEY STILL DIDN'T LEARN THEIR LESSON?
TIME ALREADY?

MOMMY!!
ACK!
OOOH!

AT THAT TIME, TEN THOUSAND MOABITE SOLDIERS DIED, AND MOAB CAME UNDER ISRAEL'S RULE.

AFTER THIS, THE PEOPLE OF ISRAEL LIVED IN PEACE FOR EIGHTY YEARS.

MMM ... THAT WAS GOOD PIZZA! OKAY, BACK TO WORK! THE NEXT JUDGE FOR ISRAEL WAS SHAMGAR ...

YAH!

SNAP!

SNIP!

RIP!

JAB!
JAB!
JAB!
JAB!
JAB!

!

SHAMGAR, YOUR FATHER WANTS YOU!

I MISSED ONE LOUSY LITTLE LEAF ...?!

STOP PLAYING! IT'S TIME TO WORSHIP OUR GODDESS!!
TAP!
YOU RANG, FATHER?

YOUR GODDESS IS A LIFELESS IDOL.
WE SHOULD ONLY WORSHIP THE LIVING GOD!

WHAT'D YOU SAY, BOY? I EVEN CHANGED MY NAME TO SERVE THE GODDESS!

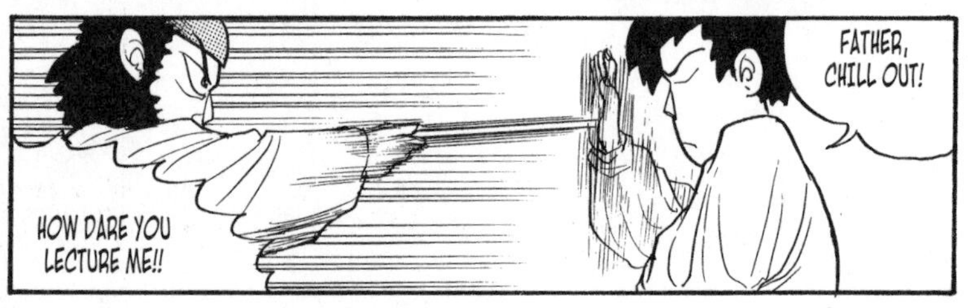
FATHER, CHILL OUT!
HOW DARE YOU LECTURE ME!!

GET OUT OF MY SIGHT! NOW!

WHATEVER YOU SAY ...

LEAVE!

THAT'S NOT GOOD ENOUGH, FATHER.
WOW ...!

... SO THE GUY LIFTED HIS SWORD AND I PRETENDED TO HEAD STRAIGHT, BUT I TURNED TO THE RIGHT!
WHO'S THAT? I HAVEN'T SEEN HIM BEFORE!
HE SAID HE FOUGHT SOME BULLFIGHTERS, AND THEY'RE ALL SCARED OF HIM NOW ...

HEY! WHAT'RE YOU TWO TALKIN' ABOUT?
JUST WONDERING IF YOU COULD BEAT SHAMGAR.

PIECE OF CAKE!

RUN! IT'S SHAMGAR!
CRACK

MOOOO-YAH!
WHAT'S THAT??

RUMBLE! RUMBLE!

RUMBLE!
?

KA-BLAM!

WHAP!

POW!

MOMMY!
휘이익
ZoOoOOooom!

I WAS BORN TO PLAY BASEBALL ...

HEY! HELP! THE PHILISTINES ARE INVADING!!
PHILISTINES?!?

WE'RE NO MATCH FOR THEIR IRON CHARIOTS!
THE AGONY! THE INHUMANITY!

DON'T BE A BUNCH OF WHINY LITTLE WIMPS! GOD IS WITH US!

THE PHILISTINES ARE SCARY! AND WHAT ARE YOU GONNA DO ... "STICK" IT TO 'EM?!

MY FAITH IS IN MORE THAN THIS STICK. IT'S IN GOD!

LET'S DRIVE OUT THE ISRAELITES AND TAKE POSSESSION OF THE LAND!

OY?

SWISSSH!

HEY KID, YOU'RE CAUSING A TRAFFIC JAM HERE ...!

I LIKE TO
JAM.

THAT'S FUNNY ... NOW GET OUTTA THE WAY!!

WE'RE HERE TO FIGHT,
NOT PLAY WITH STICKS!

WHAP!
WHAP!
OWWEEE!!
투다악

TOLD YOU
I LIKED TO
JAM ...

WHAP!
HIII-YAH!

SHAMGAR KILLED SIX HUNDRED PHILISTINE SOLDIERS AND SAVED ISRAEL. I TAKE KARATE, SO I'M TOUGH LIKE SHAMGAR!

SOME TOUGH GUY!
OKAY! OKAY! TAKE WHATEVER YOU WANT! MY CAR! MY MONEY! NEED MY PIN NUMBER? IT'S 7777! JUST PLEASE LET ME LIVE!

THE ISRAELITES CONTINUED TO FOLLOW FALSE GODS, SO GOD ALLOWED KING JABIN AND HIS GENERAL SISERA TO ATTACK ISRAEL!

FINALLY, THEY REALIZED THEIR SIN AND PRAYED TO GOD.

GOD LISTENED TO THEM AND MADE LAPPIDOTH'S WIFE, DEBORAH, A JUDGE.

DEBORAH LIVED BETWEEN RAMAH AND BETHEL IN THE HILL COUNTRY OF EPHRAIM.

SHE ALWAYS JUDGED THE ISRAELITES MOST DIFFICULT PROBLEMS ...

WHAT'S WRONG? IS THERE A PROBLEM?
SORT OF ...

I'M NOT SO SURE I CAN DO THIS, YOUR HONOR ...
FINE! THEN I'LL GO WITH YOU.

THANK YOU! THANK YOU! THANK YOU!!
MEN ...

BUT SINCE YOU'RE SO SCARED AND DIDN'T BELIEVE, SISERA WILL BE KILLED BY A WOMAN!!

GET YOUR BOYS TOGETHER AND LET'S GO!
A WOMAN? IS THAT POSSIBLE?

YOU FUNNY ...

A WOMAN IS REALLY LEADER?
YEAH, SOME CHICK NAMED DEBORAH!

YOU REAL FUNNY ...

GET CHARIOT-THINGS! WE SURROUND 'EM!

TODAY, GOD WILL GIVE US GENERAL SISERA.
START THE ATTACK!
YES, MA'AM!

OKAY, MEN ...

LET'S ROCK!

HE MUST BE A LEADER ONLY BECAUSE HE'S LOUD ...

WHAM! POW!

BOP!

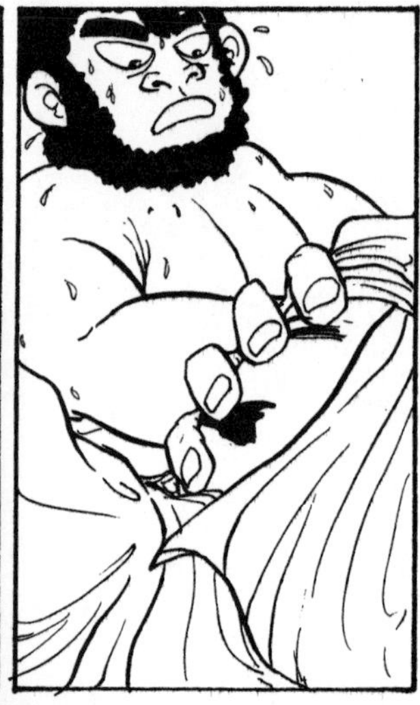

THERE'S TOO MANY!
MUST RETREAT!

DID SOMETHING JUST GO BY?
I GUESS SO!
See Sisera go!

MY, WHAT A LOVELY DAY!

PSSST ...!

NO -- NOT THE VOICES AGAIN ...!
PSSST ...!

IT ME! SISERA!
WHAT ARE YOU DOING HERE? QUICK, INTO MY TENT!

IT'S OKAY. NO ONE SAW US.
GOOD. GET WATER. NEED DRINK!

GLUG! GLUG! GLUG!

DON'T TELL. ME HIDE. ME TIRED. GO SLEEP.

HONEY, SISERA IS A BAD MAN!
BUT, KING JABIN AND OUR FAMILY ARE FRIENDS ...
ZZZZZZ

SOME FRIENDSHIP ...!

DIE, ENEMY!!
SNOOORE!

DID SISERA COME THIS WAY?

SO ISRAEL GOT RID OF JABIN AND LIVED IN PEACE FOR FORTY YEARS ...

AND THEN ONE DAY THE MIDIANITES BEGAN TO OPPRESS THE ISRAELITES ...

WHO ARE YOU?

I'M A MIDIANITE. IS THIS YOUR HARVEST? NICE JOB!
THANKS ...

OKAY THEN, I'LL BE TAKING THESE. BRING THE REST OF THE FOOD AND LIVESTOCK OUTSIDE!
?

WHY ARE YOU TAKING ALL MY STUFF?!?
YOU TALKIN' TO ME?
WHUMP!

AAAAAAH!
TAKE EVERYTHING AND KILL ANYONE WHO RESISTS!!
HELP!

PEOPLE OF ISRAEL! LET'S GO INTO THE MOUNTAINS AND LIVE IN CAVES!

AT LEAST WE'RE ABLE TO RAISE THE LIVESTOCK AND FARM ON THE MOUNTAIN.

YOU THINK YOU CAN GET AWAY THAT EASY?

TAKE THE LIVESTOCK AND BURN THE FOOD! TAKE THE WOMEN AS SLAVES!!

SOB! SOB!
GOD, FORGIVE US FOR WORSHIPING IDOLS ... AGAIN.

GIDEON WAS A YOUNG MAN WHO WORSHIPED GOD.
I KNOW GOD WILL SAVE ISRAEL!
I JUST KNOW IT!!

BUT FOR NOW, I'LL PREPARE OUR WHEAT IN THIS WINEPRESS ...

AN ANGEL!

MIGHTY WARRIOR! GOD WILL BE WITH YOU! YOU MUST SAVE ISRAEL!

BUT, I'M SMALL AND WEAK ...
FEAR NOT! FOR GOD IS WITH YOU!

THEN I WILL GIVE AN OFFERING TO GOD!

HEY! WHAT'RE YOU DOING?! YOU'RE ACTING CRAZY!!
SORRY! NO TIME TO TALK!!
우다탕탕
CRASH! BOOM! BANG!

WE'RE NOT A RESTAURANT! WHERE ARE YOU TAKING THAT FOOD?!
DON'T WORRY, MOTHER ...

HERE IS THE OFFERING. I'VE MADE MEAT, BROTH, AND BREAD WITHOUT YEAST.

PLACE THE FOOD ON THIS ROCK AND POUR THE BROTH.

FOOOM!

THE ANGEL DISAPPEARED ...!

WILL I DIE SINCE I SAW AN ANGEL?

PEACE! DO NOT BE AFRAID. YOU SHALL NOT DIE.
OH, THANK YOU, GOD!!

I WILL BUILD AN ALTAR IN THIS PLACE AND CALL IT GOD IS PEACE!

THAT NIGHT . . .

GIDEON, I AM YOUR GOD!

TEAR DOWN THE ALTAR TO BAAL AND CUT DOWN THE ASHERAH POLE!

YES, GOD! I SHALL!

I'M GOING TO DESTROY BAAL'S ALTAR AND THE ASHERAH POLE. FOLLOW ME!
WHAT IF OTHERS FIND OUT?!
WE'LL BE IN TROUBLE ...

FEAR NOT! WE HAVE GOD ON OUR SIDE!

NO PITY! DESTROY EVERYTHING!!

NOW, WE WILL BUILD AN ALTAR TO THE TRUE GOD AND GIVE AN OFFERING. WE'LL USE THE WOOD FROM THIS ALTAR AND POLE TO MAKE THE FIRE!

THE NEXT MORNING ...
SOMEONE FRIED OUR GODS!
GIDEON MUST HAVE DONE THIS!
FIND HIM! KILL HIM!!

JOASH, YOUR SON GIDEON CUT DOWN OUR GODS. GET HIM!!
IF BAAL'S REAL, LET HIM GET MY SON!

LIKE FATHER LIKE SON!!
BAAL WILL KILL GIDEON FOR SURE.

GIDEON, IT'S BEEN A FEW DAYS ... HOW DO YOU FEEL?
ARE YOU SICK? DYING ...?

WELL, NOW THAT YOU MENTION IT ...
... I'M FULL OF ENERGY AND MY APPETITE IS GROWING!
THUMP!

GIDEON, THE MIDIANITE ARMY HAS CROSSED THE JORDAN RIVER!
SEND WORD TO ALL THE TRIBES OF ISRAEL AND GATHER THE ARMY.

GIDEON, WE ONLY HAVE THIRTY-TWO THOUSAND! THAT'S ONLY HALF OF THE MIDIANITE ARMY!
HEADQUARTERS

IT WOULD BE DIFFICULT TO WIN WITH SO FEW. I MUST PRAY ...

GOD, I WILL PLACE A WOOL FLEECE ON THE THRESHING FLOOR. TOMORROW, IF THERE IS DEW ON THE FLEECE AND THE GROUND IS DRY, I WILL KNOW THAT YOU WILL SAVE ISRAEL BY MY HAND.

DEW IS ONLY ON THE FLEECE! THE GROUND IS DRY!!

THANK GOD FOR MOUNTAIN DEW!

JUST TO BE SURE ... CAN YOU WET THE GROUND AND LEAVE THE WOOL FLEECE DRY THIS TIME?

AT SUNRISE ...
DEW ONLY CAME DOWN ON THE GROUND AND THE FLEECE IS DRY!!
...

PEOPLE OF ISRAEL! I KNOW GOD IS ON OUR SIDE! FOLLOW ME!!

GIDEON, YOU HAVE TOO MANY SOLDIERS.
ARE YOU SURE? I DIDN'T SEE TOO MANY ...

DON'T TRUST IN NUMBERS! TELL WHOEVER DOESN'T WANT TO FIGHT TO GO HOME.

HEY, WHAT ARE YOU DOING?
I'M PACKING MY BAGS AND HEADING HOME!!

IF YOU GO AWOL, YOU'LL BE KILLED!
NO. GIDEON TOLD US WE CAN GO HOME IF WE WANT.

YOU SHOULDN'T GO HOME WHEN ISRAEL IS IN TROUBLE!

BUT YOU SHOULDN'T GO HOME ALONE. WAIT FOR ME TO PACK!

GOD, ONLY TEN THOUSAND ARE LEFT ...
IT IS STILL TOO MANY. LEAD THEM TO THE WATER AND WE SHALL DECREASE THE NUMBER EVEN MORE.

MEN, ALL OF YOU COME HERE AND DRINK THE WATER!

GIDEON! SEND HOME THOSE WHO KNEEL DOWN ON THEIR KNEES TO DRINK AND KEEP THOSE WHO LAP LIKE A DOG OUT OF THEIR HANDS.
OKAY!

WE ONLY HAVE THREE HUNDRED SOLDIERS NOW!
THE ENEMY HAS SIXTY THOUSAND. HMM, THAT'S ONE OF OURS FOR TWO HUNDRED OF THEIRS?

GOD, HOW CAN WE WIN WITH SO FEW AGAINST SO MANY?
TAKE YOUR SERVANT PURAH AND GO TO THE ENEMY CAMP. YOU WILL GAIN CONFIDENCE THERE.

THERE ARE SO MANY ...
LOOK, GIDEON, TWO GUARDS ARE COMING.

HEY, I HAD A STRANGE DREAM.
TELL ME, I'M GOOD WITH DREAMS.

A LOAF OF BARLEY BREAD ROLLED IN AND CRUSHED OUR TENTS!
WHAT?!? WE'RE IN TROUBLE! I THINK THAT MEANS GIDEON'S ARMY WILL CRUSH OUR ARMY ...!

OH GOD, THIS IS INCREDIBLE! THANK YOU!

WE SHALL CARRY A JAR CONTAINING A TORCH IN ONE HAND AND A TRUMPET IN THE OTHER. WE SHALL SEPARATE INTO THREE GROUPS AND SURROUND THE MIDIANITE ARMY. THEN, WHEN I BLOW THE TRUMPET, BREAK YOUR JARS AND SCREAM OUT LOUD.
작전지도
가
나
미디안 진영
다
준비물 : 나팔, 항아리 횃불

NOW GO BACK TO YOUR CAMPS AND GET READY.
I HAVE A QUESTION. IF WE ONLY BLOW TRUMPETS AND BREAK JARS, WHO'S GOING TO KILL THE MIDIANITES?
WE SHALL SEE ...

TOOT! TOOT! TOOOOT!
?
?
?

AAH!!
HELP!
WHERE ARE THEY?!
OOOF!!
LOOK OUT!
CLANG! CRASH!! TOOT! TOOOOT!! BONG! BING!! TOOT! TOOOOT!!
RUN!
FROM THE SOUND, IT'S MORE LIKE TEN MILLION!
AAAAAAAAH ...! IT'S GIDEON'S MILLION-MAN MARCH!!

AAAAAH!
I CAN'T SEE ANYTHING!
IT'S THE ENEMY!
WHERE'S MY SWORD?!
IT'S A SURPRISE ATTACK!!
ALERT!

AS THE MIDIANITE ARMY RAN AWAY IN CONFUSION, MANY WERE TRAMPLED BY ONE ANOTHER, AND OTHERS KILLED EACH OTHER BY ACCIDENT.
HEY! I'M ON YOUR TEAM!
OH YEAH! SORRY ABOUT THAT! I'M FARSIGHTED!

GO AFTER THE FLEEING SOLDIERS AND CRUSH THEM!!

WE WON!!
THANK THE LORD!!

GIDEON LED ISRAEL TO VICTORY!
I WISH I COULD MARRY GIDEON ...

CONGRATULATIONS! YOU WERE CHOSEN AS THE MOST ELIGIBLE BACHELOR IN ISRAEL!
HA! I'LL HAVE MANY BEAUTIFUL WIVES AND A LONG LIFE!

GIDEON HAS TOO MANY WIVES.
YEAH, AND HE'S GOT LIKE SEVENTY SONS ... RIGHT?

AND HIS WORST SON HAS TO BE ABIMELECH!

WHO'S TALKING ABOUT ME?

FATHER IS DEAD!
WHAT?! FATHER!?!

NOW I, ABIMELECH, WILL BE A KING!

ALL OF GIDEON'S SONS CAN'T BE KING ... RIGHT??
OF COURSE NOT. YOU SHOULD BE KING!
HECK, WE'LL EVEN GIVE YOU SEVENTY SHEKELS OF SILVER!

AHA! WITH THIS MONEY I'LL HIRE CRIMINALS TO KILL MY BROTHERS IN OPHRAH!

PUT THEM ON THE ROCK AND KILL THEM ALL!
BROTHER, PLEASE SPARE ME!
STOP!
PLEASE!

HMM! I THOUGHT I KILLED THEM ALL, BUT YOUNG JOTHAM GOT AWAY!

OOOOH ... I'M THE ONLY SURVIVOR ...!

JOTHAM, ABIMELECH FINALLY BECAME KING.

HELLO! I'M GIDEON'S YOUNGEST SON, AND I WOULD LIKE TO SAY SOMETHING!
IT'S JOTHAM!

LONG AGO, SOME TREES WERE CHOOSING A KING ...

OLIVE TREE, PLEASE BE OUR KING.
MY OIL MAKES GOD AND PEOPLE HAPPY. I CAN'T ABANDON THIS JOB TO BE KING.

FIG TREE, PLEASE BE OUR KING.
NO, I CAN'T ABANDON MY SWEET FRUIT TO BE KING OF TREES.

VINE, PLEASE BE OUR KING.

MY FRUIT AND WINE PLEASE GOD AND PEOPLE. HOW CAN I ABANDON THIS WORK TO BE KING?

THORN BUSH, PLEASE BE OUR KING.

OKAY, COME FIND SHELTER IN MY SHADE ...
... OR I'LL LET FIRE COME OUT AND BURN YOU ALL!

AND THE MORAL IS ... YOU WILL REGRET MAKING ABIMELECH YOUR KING!!

HEY THE BRAT'S BAD-MOUTHING ME!
I'LL GO GET HIM!

WHAT DO YOU MEAN YOU LOST HIM?!?

LOSE THIS ....!

GO GATHER MORE TAXES AND KILL WHOEVER RESISTS!!

HE'S PUNISHING US! THE PEOPLE WHO HELPED HIM BECOME KING?!
HE'S A THORN TREE JUST LIKE JOTHAM SAID!

ABIMELECH IS A LOW-LIFE HOOD. LET'S GET A REAL KING!
YOU'RE RIGHT. LET'S ELECT GAAL AS KING!

WHAT?! THE PEOPLE OF SHECHEM BETRAYED ME AND MADE GAAL KING?!

I'LL KILL THEM ALL! EVEN THEIR CHILDREN!!

KILL THEM! CRUSH THEM! KILL THEM GOOD!

WHAT? THEY'RE IN THE TOWER OF SHECHEM?!

BURN IT AND POUR SALT ON THE FIELDS TO KILL THEIR CROPS!

WE BURNED THE TOWER UP!!
NOW, LET'S GO CATCH THE PEOPLE OF THEBEZ AND BURN THOSE BETRAYERS TOO!

WHAT? ALL THE PEOPLE OF THEBEZ ARE ON THE TOP OF THE TOWER?!

IT'S TIME FOR ANOTHER BBQ PARTY! MOO-WAH-HA-HA ...!

THIS TIME I'LL LIGHT THE FIRE MYSELF!

AH, THESE MATCHES ARE HORRIBLE! WHAT ARE THEY ... WET?

ULP! HE'S TRYING TO LIGHT THE FIRE!!!

HEY YOU! BEWARE OF FALLING ROCKS!

YES, SHE HAS WONDERFUL FORM. SHE'S WINDING UP, AND HERE'S THE PITCH!
WHAT ARM STRENGTH! SHE'S INCREDIBLE!
SBC 중계석

IT LOOKS LIKE A FASTBALL! GRAVITY SURE HELPS A MILLSTONE FLY!
HER FOLLOW-THROUGH IS PERFECT! THAT'S THE RESULT OF YEARS OF TRAINING!!

IT'S IN THE STRIKE ZONE!
WOW! SHE'S READY FOR THE PROS!

WELL ... ANY FINAL THOUGHTS?
ABSOLUTELY! I THINK THAT WOMAN WILL GO DOWN IN THE ISRAELITE HALL OF FAME. A PERFECT PITCH THAT WILL BE REMEMBERED FOR A LONG TIME TO COME!
WE NOW RETURN TO OUR NORMALLY SCHEDULED MANGA ...

HEY, I'M NOT DEAD YET ...!

HEY YOU WITH THE SWORD, COME HERE!
M-ME?

MY HEAD IS CRACKED AND I'M GOING TO DIE. PLEASE KILL ME WITH THAT SWORD. IF NOT, I SHALL BE RIDICULED FOR BEING KILLED BY A WOMAN.

I ... I CAN'T BELIEVE ... I WAS ... DONE IN ... BY A ... FASTBALL!!

AFTER THIS, THE ISRAELITES WORSHIPED MANY IDOLS (AGAIN).
OH, MOLECH!

GOD GATHERED THE PHILISTINE AND AMORITE ARMIES -- CAUSING GREAT SUFFERING FOR EIGHTEEN YEARS.
ISRAEL IS OURS!
HEY, I'M BORED. LET'S GO BOTHER THE ISRAELITES!

GOD! PLEASE FORGIVE US AND SAVE US AGAIN!!!

PEOPLE OF ISRAEL! HOW MANY TIMES DOES THIS MAKE? GO ASK YOUR IDOLS TO SAVE YOU.

BUT ... THE IDOLS DON'T HAVE ANY POWER TO SAVE US!
THEN WHY DO YOU KEEP WORSHIPING THEM?!

WE'RE SILLY LITTLE HUMANS. NOW, PLEASE SAVE US. WE'LL CRUSH THE IDOLS!

OH NO! HERE COMES THE MOABITE ARMY OVER NEAR GILEAD.
I GUESS WE'RE ON OUR OWN ...

WHO WILL BE OUR COMMANDER AND FIGHT THE AMMONITES?

WHOEVER WINS WILL BECOME THE HEAD OF ISRAEL.
I KNOW PEOPLE WILL FIGHT EACH OTHER TO BE COMMANDER OF THE ARMY ... SHOULD I PICK BY THEIR WEIGHT OR HOLD A LOTTERY ...?

ALL RIGHT, THOSE OF YOU WHO WANT TO BECOME THE COMMANDER, PLEASE COME FORWARD!!!

UH-OH! WHERE DID THEY ALL GO?

COWARDS ... THEY ALL RAN AWAY IN FEAR OF THEIR LIVES! IF I WERE YOUNGER I COULD BECOME THE COMMANDER...!!

WAIT A SEC! I'M NOT DEAD YET! WHY NOT ME?!?

LET'S GO!

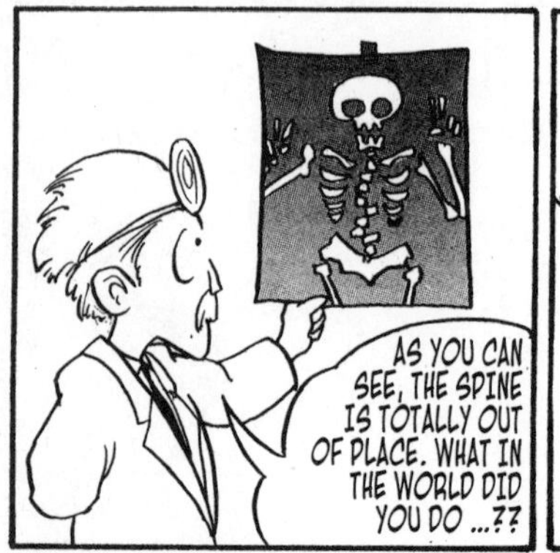
AS YOU CAN SEE, THE SPINE IS TOTALLY OUT OF PLACE. WHAT IN THE WORLD DID YOU DO ...??

I WAS PRACTICING A LITTLE KARATE, THAT'S ALL ...

YOU SHOULD'VE CALLED JEPHTHAH. I HEARD HE'S A GREAT WARRIOR ...
BUT DIDN'T HIS FAMILY BANISH HIM?

MAYBE ... BUT HE'S PROBABLY THE ONLY ONE WHO CAN FIGHT THE AMMONITES!!

LET'S GO FIND HIM ...

WAIT! I NEED TO USE THE RESTROOM!
DON'T WORRY. YOU'LL HAVE THAT CAST OFF IN SIX WEEKS. SHOW A LITTLE SELF-CONTROL ...

JEPHTHAH, PLEASE HELP US. WE NEED YOU!
BUT YOU BANISHED ME!

WE WERE WRONG. IF YOU DEFEAT THE ENEMY, WE'LL MAKE YOU A JUDGE.
REALLY? THIS ISN'T A TRICK?

OKAY. LET'S DO THIS!!

WE'RE SAVED! DOES THIS MEAN I CAN GET MY CAST OFF SOONER?
NO.

THIS LOOKS LIKE A GOOD ARMY.

BUT WE WILL WIN ONLY IF GOD HELPS US. LET US PRAY ...

DEAR LORD, PLEASE GIVE THE AMMONITES INTO MY HANDS, AND GIVE YOUR PEOPLE A VICTORY!

PREPARE YOURSELF! STAY LOOSE. GET READY ...

ATTACK!!

ACK!!

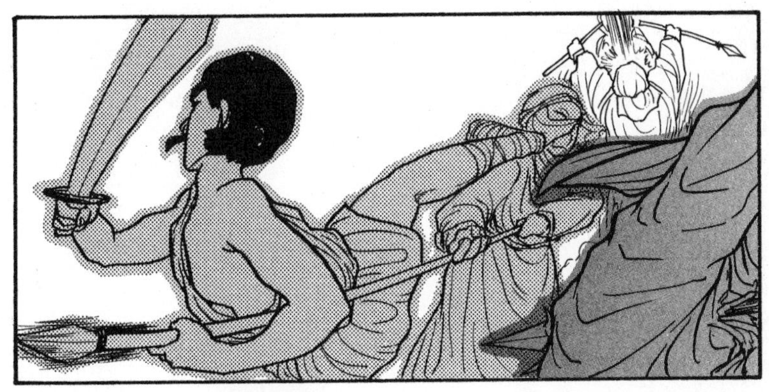

WE GIVE UP! PLEASE, SPARE OUR LIVES!

IT IS GOD'S GREAT VICTORY! LET'S GO HOME!!

AND NOW, HERE COMES THE STAR OF THE BOOK OF JUDGES ... SAMSON! SAMSON MEANS "SUN" OR "BRIGHTNESS" IN HEBREW.

IN KOREAN, SAMSON MEANS "THREE HANDS" ...
WE'RE NOT IN KOREA!
AND I'M NOT SAMSON!

THE LAND OF ZORAH

MANOAH'S HOUSE

WHY ARE WE WITHOUT A CHILD ...?

OH! AN ANGEL!

DO NOT DRINK WINE OR BEER OR EAT ANYTHING UNCLEAN, BECAUSE YOU SHALL HAVE A SON. YOU MUST NEVER CUT HIS HAIR, BECAUSE HE WILL BE A NAZIRITE.
1004

HE WILL SAVE ISRAEL FROM THE PHILISTINES.

POOF!
OH!

OH, MANOAH, MY HUSBAND! AN ANGEL APPEARED TO ME!
REALLY? LET ME KNOW NEXT TIME IT SHOWS UP ...

HONEY --! THE ANGEL!!
OKAY -- I'LL GIVE AN OFFERING TO GOD, ALL RIGHT?

WE WOULD LIKE TO GIVE OUR GOAT AS AN OFFERING TO GOD.
VERY NICE ...

WOW! THE ANGEL IS RIDING THE FLAME UP INTO THE SKY!

NINE MONTHS LATER ...
I THINK IT'S TIME!

IT WAS TIME ...
WAAAH!

YOU DID A SUPER JOB! LET'S NAME HIM CLARK!
I THINK I LIKE THE NAME SAMSON BETTER.

SO SAMSON GREW ...
GET MY BALL!

HE BECAME A STRONG YOUNG MAN.
I'M IN LOVE!
I MET A PHILISTINE GIRL I WANT TO MARRY!!
YOU MET A WHAT?!

AREN'T THERE ANY WOMEN IN ISRAEL? PHILISTINE WOMEN DON'T WORSHIP GOD!!
I STILL WANT TO MARRY HER, FATHER! PLEASE, GO TO TIMNAH WITH ME!

IT'S THE MUSIC THESE KIDS LISTEN TO THESE DAYS ...!
YEEHAW! I-AM-GONNA-GET-MARRIED!!

AAAAAH!!

HIYA.

QUICK! RUN AWAY!
HEY! THIS HIPPIE ISN'T EVEN AFRAID!

MUST BE BLIND OR SOME-THING. WELL, THIS'LL DIRTY HIS LOINCLOTH ...!

ROAR!

HE MUST BE BLIND AND DEAF! THIS IS REALLY GETTING ANNOYING!!

HEY, GET OUT OF THE WAY, KITTY! I'VE GOT VERY SERIOUS BUSINESS TO ATTEND TO!!

KITTY ...? KITTY?!?!?

G-R-ROWWWL!!

SNAP!

YOU SHOULD GET THAT LOOKED AT. YOU'LL PROBABLY NEED STITCHES ...

AFTER FEW DAYS ...
I'M SO HAPPY ... TODAY, I'M GETTING MARRIED!!

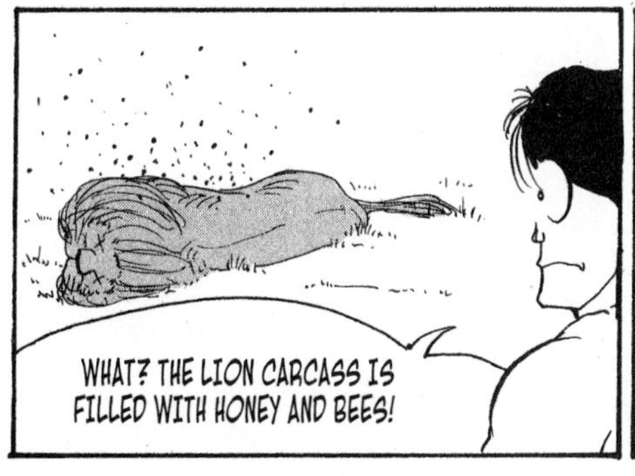
WHAT? THE LION CARCASS IS FILLED WITH HONEY AND BEES!

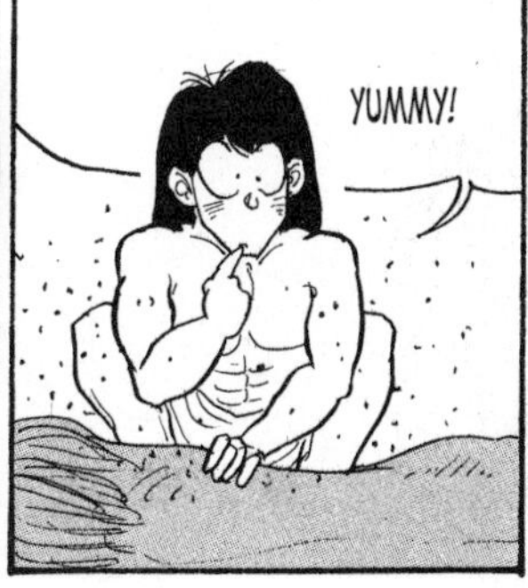
YUMMY!

MOM! DAD! I BROUGHT HOME SOME HONEY!
THAT'S SO SWEET OF YOU!
THE MORE PEOPLE, THE BETTER THE PARTY!!
TOOTHPICKS, ANYONE?
I'LL TELL YOU A RIDDLE, AND IF YOU SOLVE IT IN ONE WEEK, I'LL GIVE YOU THIRTY LINEN SHIRTS. BUT, IF YOU CAN'T, YOU MUST GIVE ME THE SHIRTS.
OKAY! TELL US THE RIDDLE!!
"OUT OF THE EATER, SOMETHING TO EAT; OUT OF THE STRONG, SOMETHING SWEET." WHAT IS THE EATER? WHAT IS THE SWEET?

THAT'S HARD!
I CAN'T FIGURE IT OUT!
I GOT NOTHIN'!
I REALLY CAN'T FIGURE IT OUT!
I'M GOING TO HAVE SAMSON'S WIFE GET THE ANSWER!

IF YOU CAN'T GET THE ANSWER FROM SAMSON, I'M GOING TO BLOW YOUR HOUSE UP!!

HONEY, TELL ME THE ANSWER.
YOU'LL HAVE TO WAIT WITH THE REST OF THEM.

BOO-HOO! YOU DON'T LOVE ME ANYMORE! YOU CAN'T EVEN TELL ME THE ANSWER TO A RIDDLE?!!

OKAY! I CAN'T STAND THE CRYING ...! I'LL TELL YOU, BUT YOU CAN'T TELL ANYONE ELSE.

"THE EATER IS THE LION, AND SWEET IS THE HONEY!" THAT IS THE ANSWER!!

COWARDS! THEY USED MY WIFE ... BUT I'LL KEEP MY PROMISE!
CRACK

ALONG THE ASHKELON ROAD ...
HERE COMES A PHILISTINE!
I'M SO SLEEPY!

ONLY TWENTY-NINE SHIRTS TO GO!

HELLO, CHEATERS! HERE ARE THE THIRTY SHIRTS I PROMISED!!

IN OTHER NEWS ... THIRTY BODIES WERE FOUND WITHOUT THEIR SHIRTS ON. POLICE SAY THIS MUST BE THE WORK OF A CRAZY MAN ...!

WE'RE IN TROUBLE! THE PHILISTINES ARE INVADING!!

GIVE US SAMSON AND WE'LL LEAVE.
WHY ARE YOU DOING THIS?

HEY SAMSON! WE'RE ALL GOING TO DIE THANKS TO YOU!
ALL RIGHT, I'LL GO WITH THEM ...

FINALLY OUR PROBLEMS ARE SOLVED.
HA! THIS WAS EASIER THAN WE THOUGHT!

ISRAEL IS FOOLISH TO THINK WE'LL LEAVE THEM ALONE JUST BECAUSE SAMSON IS GONE!!

REALLY ...?!

SNAP!
WHAT? HE BROKE THE ROPE?! KILL HIM QUICKLY!!!

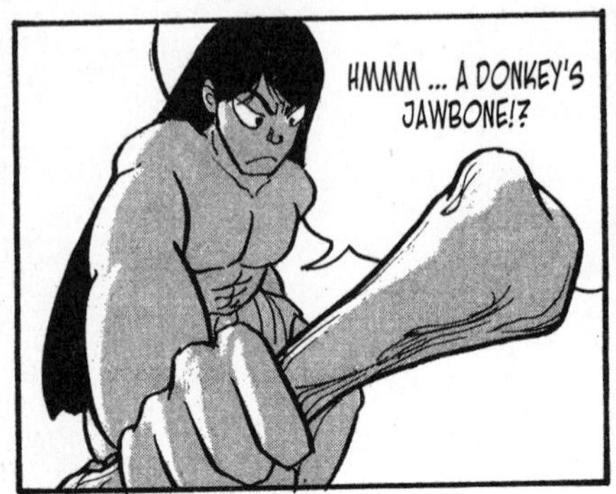
HMMM ... A DONKEY'S JAWBONE!?

WHACK!

DADDY! DADDY! I SEE FLYING PEOPLE!
YEAH, RIGHT ...

IT'S RAINING MEN ...!
POW!
POW!
POW!
POW!
POW!

AFTER KILLING ONE THOUSAND PHILISTINES ... I'M THIRSTY!!

PLEASE! I'M THIRSTY!! GIVE ME WATER!!!

WOW! SPRING WATER! THANKS, GOD!!

I KNEW IT! I'M BEING TREATED DIFFERENTLY BECAUSE OF MY STRENGTH.
MASTER, PLEASE BECOME OUR JUDGE!

I HEARD SAMSON BECAME A JUDGE.
IT WILL BE HARD TO ATTACK ISRAEL NOW.

YOU DON'T KNOW ANYTHING. EVEN SAMSON HAS A WEAKNESS!
A WEAKNESS?

SAMSON HAS A WEAK SPOT FOR WOMEN! WE NEED TO GET HIS GIRLFRIEND, DELILAH, ON OUR SIDE.

DING DONG!

SORRY, WE ALREADY GAVE AT THE OFFICE!

I HAVE A SMALL GIFT FOR YOU.
WELL, WHY DIDN'T YOU SAY SO?

LET ME GET STRAIGHT TO THE POINT. IF YOU FIND OUT THE SECRET SOURCE OF SAMSON'S STRENGTH, WE'LL GIVE YOU ELEVEN HUNDRED SHEKELS OF SILVER.

NO PROBLEM! HAVE THOSE SHEKELS READY. I'LL LEARN HIS SECRET IN NO TIME!

SAMSON, LOVE OF MY LIFE ...
YES?

WHAT'S THE SECRET SOURCE OF YOUR STRENGTH?
UMM ... IF YOU TIE ME UP WITH SEVEN NEW LEATHER THONGS, I CAN'T USE MY STRENGTH.

HMM ... I'LL TIE HIM UP WITH THONGS AND THEN ...

HONEY! THE PHILISTINES ARE COMING!!

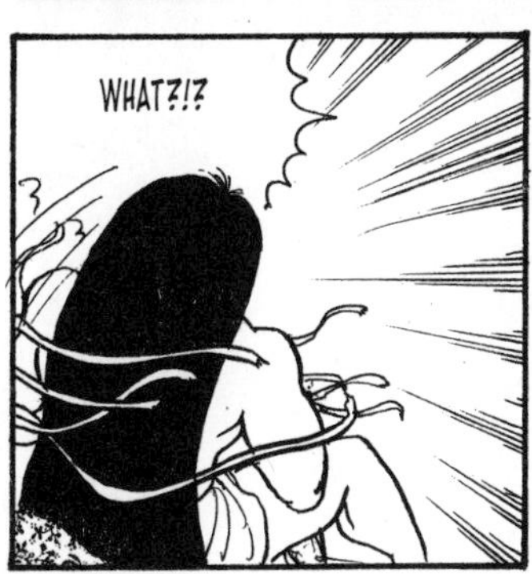
WHAT?!?

OKAY -- I'LL TELL YOU THE TRUTH THIS TIME. IF YOU TIE ME WITH NEW ROPES, I CAN'T MOVE.

SWEETY-PIE! THE PHILISTINES ARE COMING!!

WHAT?! REALLY!?!

SOB! YOU'RE SUCH A LIAR. I'M GOING TO KILL MYSELF!
I CAN'T STAND WOMEN CRYING ...!

THIS IS THE TRUTH ... IF I CUT MY HAIR, I WILL BE WEAK.

THE MOST EXPENSIVE HAIRCUT IN HISTORY!

HONEY, THE PHILISTINES ARE HERE!!
WHAT?! THE PHILISTINE'S ARE HERE?!?

FOOLS!!
I THOUGHT SHE DID IT RIGHT THIS TIME!!

KA-POW!

WAIT A SEC! I HIT YOU ...!
ARE YOU KIDDING?

IS THIS A DREAM? MAYBE I'LL TRY AGAIN ...

BAM!

IT KINDA' TICKLES ...!

OH, NO!! MY HAIR ...!!!

HA! LOOK AT YOU!! TAKE HIS EYES OUT AND PUT HIM IN JAIL!!!

GOD, PLEASE FORGIVE ME ...

AS TIME WENT ON, SAMSON'S HAIR GREW LONGER AND LONGER ...

WE CELEBRATE OUR GOD DAGON TODAY!
BRING SAMSON IN TO ENTERTAIN US!

WHERE'S YOUR STRENGTH?!
OPEN YOUR EYES!

GOD, GIVE ME THE STRENGTH TO PAY THEM BACK FOR TAKING MY EYES!

C-C-CRACK!
ERRRR!!!

AAAAAAAH! EEEEEEEK!!!
KAAA-BOOOOOOM!!!

SAMSON KILLED MORE PHILISTINES IN HIS DEATH THAN IN HIS LIFE.

SAMSON'S BROTHERS BROUGHT HIS BODY AND BURIED HIM IN HIS FATHER'S TOMB.
YOUR SISTER CALLED. SHE WANTS HER SHIRT BACK.

ONCE AGAIN, THE TRIBES WERE AT WAR, BUT THIS TIME IT WAS AGAINST ONE OF THEIR OWN ...
THE BENJAMITES ATTACKED US ...
THEY KILLED THE WOMAN I LOVE ...

I'LL TELL ALL OF ISRAEL WHAT HAS HAPPENED HERE!!!

THOSE BENJAMITE PUNKS DID A HORRIBLE THING!!
LET'S GATHER AN ARMY!!

OUR ARMY WILL MARCH TO GIBEAH WHERE THE TRIBE OF BENJAMIN LIVES!!

TRIBE OF BENJAMIN! YOU HAVE COMMITTED A HORRIBLE SIN! SEND OUT THE MURDERERS WHO DID THIS!!
WHO DIED AND MADE YOU GOD?
YOU CAN'T JUDGE US!

ENOUGH TALK! ATTACK!!
YOU WILL TASTE THE POWER OF THE BENJAMITES!
WE WILL NOT MISS WITH OUR SLING SHOTS!!

ZIP!
ZIP!
ZIP!

WHAP!
OWW!
OWW!
WHAP!
WHAP!
OWW!

RETREAT! RETREAT!!

SIR, WE LOST TWENTY THOUSAND MEN.
LET US PRAY, FAST, AND GIVE AN OFFERING!

GOD, GIVE US THE STRENGTH!

YOU WILL WIN IF YOU FIGHT TOMORROW.

AFTER THIS, THE OTHER TRIBES FOUND WIVES FOR THE SURVIVING SIX HUNDRED BENJAMITES AND THEY LIVED IN PEACE ...

RUTH

BETHLEHEM

THE HOUSE OF ELIMELECH
S-S-SCRAPE!

S-S-SCRAPE! SCRAPE!
COOKIES

HMPH!

THE LAST COOKIE CRUMBS. IT'S ALL WE HAVE TO EAT ...
COOKI

MAHLON, I'M HUNGRY ...
MOM, KILION'S HUNGRY ...!
THE KIDS ARE HUNGRY ...!
STOP, NAOMI! YOU'RE MAKING ME HUNGRY!

DAYS LATER ...
OUR CHILDREN PASSED OUT FROM HUNGER ...!

ALL RIGHT! ALL RIGHT! I'M ABOUT TO MAKE A VERY IMPORTANT DECISION ...

WE'RE GOING TO MOAB TO FIND SOME FOOD!!

I DON'T WANT TO LEAVE BETHLEHEM ... I HEARD ALL THE PEOPLE OF MOAB WORSHIP IDOLS!
SO, YOU'D RATHER WE ALL STARVE TO DEATH?

DO AS YOU WISH ...
LET'S PACK AND LEAVE NOW!

HAVE A NICE VACATION! DRIVE SAFE, ELIMELECH!
WE'LL BE BACK... IF WE SURVIVE!

ARE WE THERE YET?
DON'T KNOW. ARE WE THERE YET?
HONEY, THE KIDS WANT TO KNOW ...?
DOES IT LOOK LIKE WE'RE THERE YET?!?

EXTREME TENT MAKEOVER
MOAB EDITION
WELL, WE'RE FINISHED WITH OUR HOUSE. LET'S START A BUSINESS!
YES, LET'S BUILD A BETTER LIFE!
BUILDER -- ELIMELECH

ANOTHER HARD DAY AT WORK ...!
IT'S DADDY --!!

YOU'RE WORKING TOO HARD. TAKE SOME TIME OFF.
I CAN'T, HONEY! WE NEED THE MONEY ...!

SO DIZZY ...

OH, MY!!
CLUMP!

DOCTOR ...
HE'S OVERWORKED AND UNDERFED ... YOU SHOULD PREPARE YOURSELF ...!

NAOMI, HONEY ...! I'M NOT GONNA MAKE IT ...! RAISE MAHLON AND KILION WELL ...

AND SO, THE KIDS GREW ...
IT'S TIME FOR YOU BOYS TO FIND WIVES. ANYONE IN MIND?

I'D LIKE TO MARRY OUR NEIGHBOR ORPAH.

KILION, ORPAH'S HOUSEHOLD WORSHIPS IDOLS!
I'LL HELP THEM BELIEVE IN GOD!

MAHLON, WHO DO YOU LIKE?
GETTING MARRIED! GETTING MARRIED!

I LIKE RUTH WHO LIVES IN THE NEXT TOWN ...!
~SHE'S CUTE.

THAT PRETTY GIRL? CAN YOU HELP HER BELIEVE IN GOD TOO?
YEAH! I'M ALREADY TEACHING RUTH ABOUT GOD

THAT'S GREAT!
YOU'LL MARRY HER
NEXT MONTH!

SOON, NAOMI BECAME RUTH AND ORPAH'S MOTHER-IN-LAW ...

UNFORTUNATELY, KILION AND MAHLON SOON DIED FROM ILLNESS ...
OOOHHH! OOOHHH!

GIRLS, YOU'RE STILL YOUNG! REMARRY! I'M GOING HOME ...

WE ARE YOUR FAMILY NOW. WE'LL FOLLOW YOU!!

NO, DON'T SACRIFICE YOUR LIFE FOR ME. GO HOME TO YOUR FATHER!

WELL ...

GOOD-BYE SISTER ORPAH!
GOOD-BYE SISTER RUTH! HAVE FUN IN BETHLEHEM!
FIND A GOOD HUSBAND! HAVE A NICE LIFE!
YOU SHOULD LEAVE TOO ...
I'LL NEVER LEAVE YOU! NO MATTER WHAT!

YOU HAVE YOUR WHOLE LIFE AHEAD OF YOU!

I DON'T LIKE IDOL WORSHIPERS. I WANT TO GO AND WORSHIP GOD WITH YOU!!

HMM?

YOU'RE LETTING ME GO WITH YOU?!
IF THAT'S WHAT YOU REALLY WANT! FOLLOW ME!!

WELCOME TO BETHLEHEM ...!

AIN'T SHE ELIMELECH'S WIFE, NAOMI?
WHY'S SHE COMIN' BACK WITHOUT HER MEN?
NAOMI! HOWDY! WHAT HAPPENED TO YOUR FAMILY? WHO'S THIS?

NAOMI MEANS "HAPPY." YOU SHOULD CALL ME MARA, WHICH MEANS "BITTER." OOH!

I LEFT THIS HOLY LAND FOR A LAND OF IDOLS. MY HUSBAND AND MY SONS ALL DIED!
SO SAD ...

MY DAUGHTER-IN-LAW HERE FOLLOWED ME TO WORSHIP GOD.
HI, I'M RUTH!

DOWNRIGHT NICE ... AND A LOOKER TOO!
WHY THANK YOU, YOU STRANGE OLD MEN ...!

THIS IS WHERE WE USED TO STARVE ...

THIS IS OUR HOUSE! WE'LL NOT SURRENDER!!

SURE, WE WERE MESSY, BUT THESE CLEAN FREAKS ARE DRIVING ME CRAZY! ARE WE JUST GONNA SCURRY AROUND AND WIGGLE OUR TAILS? I DON'T THINK SO!!

DON'T GET CRAZY, MICKEY. LET'S SET A FEW TRAPS AND SEE HOW THEY LIKE IT ...

THERE ARE ONLY TWO OF THEM AND SIX HUNDRED OF US!
WE MUST DEFEND THIS ABBEY ...!!
I WANT A MASK. ...

CREEEAK!

I THINK WE'RE ALMOST FINISHED CLEANING.

SEE HOW WE RUN!
SAVE YOURSELF!!

I THOUGHT I HEARD SOMETHING ...?

THE THREE BLIND ONES DIDN'T MAKE IT OUT ...
THEY DON'T KNOW THAT.

THE CLEANING'S FINALLY FINISHED ...!
BRUSH! BRUSH!

WHY DON'T WE HAVE DINNER NOW?
YES, MOTHER. WHAT WOULD YOU LIKE TO EAT?

OH, WE HAVE NOTHING TO EAT ...
MUST BRING BACK MEMORIES?

I'M TOO TIRED TO EAT ...!
ME TOO!

THE NEXT MORNING ...
I'LL GET THE LEFTOVER GRAINS FROM THE FIELD.

I WAS ALWAYS GOOD AT FINDING THINGS ...

HELLO, MR. BOAZ!
YOU'RE DOING A GREAT JOB.

CAN'T LET ANY LEFTOVER GRAIN GO TO WASTE. GOTTA GET 'EM ALL ...
WHO IS THAT WOMAN?
THAT'S RUTH, THE DAUGHTER-IN-LAW NAOMI BROUGHT FROM THE LAND OF MOAB.

SHE IS ...? PLEASE, BRING HER TO ME.

AM I IN TROUBLE?
NO, IT'S NOTHING LIKE THAT ...

YOU ARE WELCOME TO STAY IN THIS FIELD. PICK UP ALL YOU WANT AND DRINK THE WATER THE WORKERS BRING.

THANK YOU FOR YOUR KIND OFFER, SIR.

I HEARD WHAT YOU'VE DONE FOR NAOMI. YOU ARE THE KIND ONE.

LEAVE A LOT OF GRAIN SO RUTH HAS PLENTY TO PICK UP!!
YES, MASTER!!

WOW!

WHERE DID YOU GET ALL OF THIS GRAIN?

A MAN NAMED BOAZ LET ME PICK ALL THIS!
MAY GOD BLESS HIS KIND SOUL!

LATER ...
YOU LOOK LONELY. YOU SHOULD MARRY BOAZ.

HE'S A LITTLE OLD FOR ME, BUT HE BELIEVES IN GOD. SO I WILL.

SO RUTH MARRIED BOAZ AND THEY HAD A SON WHO WOULD BE THE GRANDFATHER OF KING DAVID!
BOAZ - OBED - JESSE - DAVID
END OF RUTH

WAIT! DON'T LEAVE ME! I'LL DRAW ANOTHER BOOK!

STUDENT BY DAY,
NINJA AT NIGHT!

I Was an Eighth-Grade Ninja

Available Now!

My Double-Edged Life

Available Now!

Child of Destiny

Available February 2008!

The Argon Deception

Available May 2008!

AVAILABLE AT YOUR LOCAL BOOKSTORE!

VOLUMES 5-8 COMING SOON!

GRAPHIC NOVELS

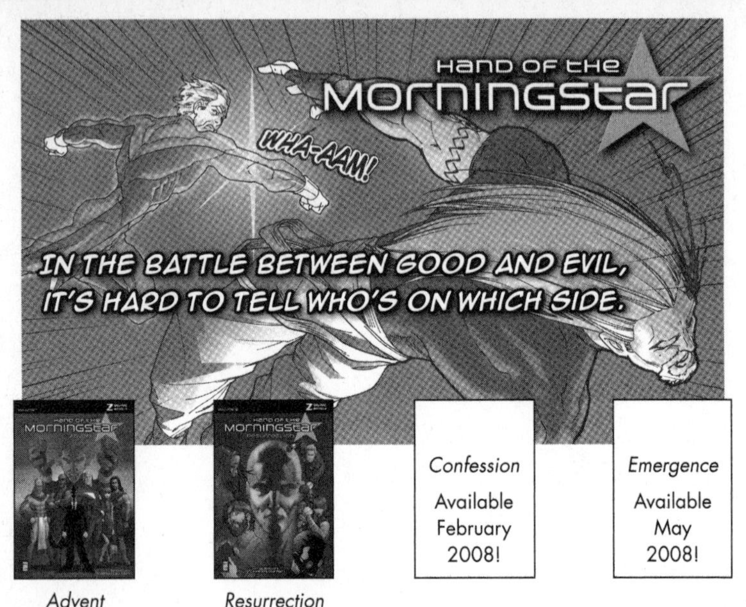

Advent

Available Now!

Resurrection

Available Now!

Confession

Available February 2008!

Emergence

Available May 2008!

AVAILABLE AT YOUR LOCAL BOOKSTORE!

VOLUMES 5-8 COMING SOON!

ZONDERVAN®

We want to hear from you. Please send your comments
about this book to us in care of zreview@zondervan.com. Thank you.

Grand Rapids, MI 49530
www.zonderkidz.com